Katie Kazoo, Switcheroo

Don't Be Such a Turkey!

GROSSET & DUNLAP
Published by the Penguin Group
Penguin Group (USA) Inc., 375 Hudson Street, New York,
New York 10014, USA
Penguin Group (Canada), 90 Eglinton Avenue East, Suite 700, Toronto,
Ontario M4P 2Y3, Canada
(a division of Pearson Penguin Canada Inc.)
Penguin Books Ltd., 80 Strand, London WC2R 0RL, England
Penguin Group Ireland, 25 St. Stephen's Green, Dublin 2,
Ireland(a division of Penguin Books Ltd.)
Penguin Group (Australia), 250 Camberwell Road, Camberwell, Victoria 3124,
Australia(a division of Pearson Australia Group Pty. Ltd.)
Penguin Books India Pvt. Ltd., 11 Community Centre, Panchsheel Park,
New Delhi—110 017, India
Penguin Group (NZ), 67 Apollo Drive, Rosedale, North Shore 0632,
New Zealand (a division of Pearson New Zealand Ltd.)
Penguin Books (South Africa) (Pty.) Ltd., 24 Sturdee Avenue,
Rosebank, Johannesburg 2196, South Africa

Penguin Books Ltd., Registered Offices:
80 Strand, London WC2R 0RL, England

Library of Congress Control Number: 2010003992

ISBN 978-0-448-45448-1 10 9 8 7 6 5 4 3 2 1

For Pepper, who gets
the leftover turkey.—N.K.

For New York City — where magic happened
and our wish came true!—J&W

Katie Kazoo, Switcheroo

Don't Be Such a Turkey!

by Nancy Krulik • illustrated by John & Wendy

Grosset & Dunlap
An Imprint of Penguin Group (USA) Inc.

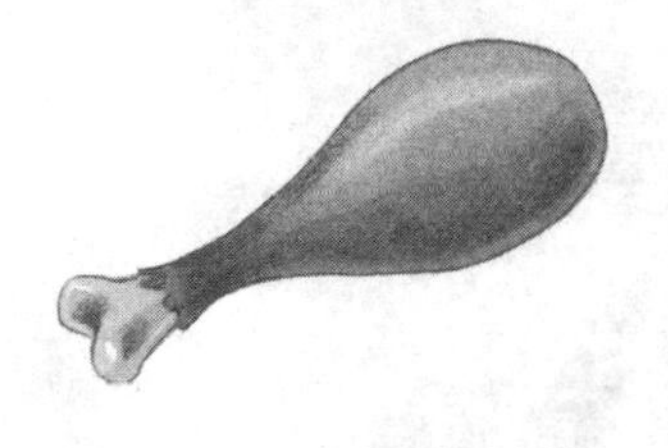

Chapter 1

"Good morrow, young ones," Mr. Guthrie greeted the kids of class 4A on Monday morning. "How do you fare on this fine day?"

Katie Carew waved hi as she came into the classroom. Her teacher was wearing a white shirt, a flat black hat, and short black pants. Katie wasn't totally surprised that Mr. Guthrie was dressed like that. Her teacher was always dressing up in weird costumes. This was nothing compared to the time he'd put on ears and a tail to dress like a mouse when the class was learning about animals that only came out at night. Or when he'd greeted the kids dressed as a daisy, with white petals all around his face,

when they were studying flowering plants. Now that had been *really* strange.

"What's with the shorts, Mr. G.?" Kadeem Carter asked the teacher.

"Do you mean my breeches?" Mr. G. asked. "The men all wear breeches in our village."

Katie had a feeling Mr. G. didn't mean Cherrydale when he said *our village*. So what exactly was he talking about?

"Whoa! Check it out!" Kevin Camilleri said as he walked into the classroom. Katie looked to where Kevin was pointing. There was a huge gray rock in the corner of the room. Well, actually it wasn't a real rock. It was a piece of Styrofoam painted gray to *look* like a giant rock.

Now Katie knew what was going on. Thanksgiving was only a week and a half away. So that must mean . . .

"That's Plymouth Rock!" Katie exclaimed. "We must be studying the Pilgrims!"

"Huzzah!" Mr. G. shouted excitedly. "Good thinking, Katie Kazoo."

Katie giggled. She loved when her teacher used the way-cool nickname her friend George had given her back in third grade.

"But we are not only studying the Pilgrims," Mr. G. continued. "The Wampanoags will also be part of our learning adventure."

"The Wampa-whats?" Kevin asked.

"The Wampanoags," Mandy Banks told him. "They were the Native Americans who lived near the Pilgrims."

"Huzzah, Mandy!" Mr. G. cheered.

Katie laughed. *Huzzah* was a very funny-sounding word. It was also very cheerful. She figured it had to mean congratulations or something like that.

"Can we decorate our beanbags now?" Emma Stavros asked Mr. G.

"Of course," Mr. G. said. "Go forth and decorate."

Katie couldn't wait to start decorating her beanbag chair. That was always the most fun part of starting a new learning adventure.

Mr. G. called all lessons learning adventures. And he let the kids sit in beanbags instead of at desks so they could be comfortable while they were learning. Mr. G. wasn't at all like other teachers.

Katie went over to the crafts section of the classroom and grabbed some pretty feathers.

"Are you making a turkey for your beanbag, Katie?" Kevin asked her.

Katie shook her head. "It's going to be a Native American headdress."

"Katie would never make a turkey," Emma Weber told Kevin. "She doesn't eat turkey."

Katie nodded. That was true. She was a vegetarian. Her Thanksgiving dinner was going to be mashed potatoes and tofu that was made to look like turkey slices. Her dad called it tofurkey.

"I'll eat anything," Kevin said. "In fact, I'm going to turn my beanbag into a massive Thanksgiving dinner." He took a piece of red tissue paper and rolled it up into a ball. "Starting with this tomato."

Katie giggled. Kevin was the tomato-eating king of the fourth grade. No meal was complete for him unless there were tomatoes. She bet he even ate tomatoes for dessert!

Kadeem looked up from the *Mayflower*

boat he was building with construction paper on his beanbag. "Hey, do you guys know why the turkey crossed the road?" he asked.

"Why?" Andrew Epstein asked.

"Because it was the chicken's day off," Kadeem answered. He started laughing at his own joke. Then he got quiet and looked sad.

Katie knew why Kadeem was sad. Usually when he told a joke, his friend George would tell one right back. And then Kadeem would tell one. They would go back and forth. Mr. G. called it a Kadeem-George joke-off.

But George and his family had moved away. Now Kadeem had no one to joke with. Everybody missed George.

Then, suddenly, Emma W. began to giggle. "Hey, Kadeem, if the Pilgrims were alive today, do you know what they'd be famous for?" she asked.

"What?" Kadeem asked.

"Their age!" Emma W. said. She burst out laughing. So did everyone else. That was pretty funny. The Pilgrims would definitely be very old if they were still alive!

Katie stared at Emma W. in amazement. Usually she was so quiet. But now, here she was telling a joke in front of the whole class. Amazing!

"Oh yeah?" Kadeem said, sounding much happier now that he had someone to tell jokes with. "Well, if April showers bring May flowers, what do May flowers bring?"

"Pilgrims," Emma W. told him. "That's such an old joke, I bet the Pilgrims told it to each other on the boat!"

Wow! A Kadeem-Emma W. joke-off. Who would have thought *that* could happen? Of course, just about anything could happen in class 4A.

"Hurry up and decorate, ye young dudes," Mr. G. said with a smile. "I have a special surprise planned."

"What's the surprise?" Emma S. asked Mr. G.

"If I told you, it wouldn't *be* a surprise,"

Mr. G. said. "But here's a hint. It involves sticks and strings."

Katie had no idea what that meant. Neither did anyone else. When you had a teacher like Mr. G., a stick and a string could be for anything!

Chapter 2

"Okay, everyone, grab a stick," Mr. G. said as he dumped a big pile of sticks in the middle of the field behind the school.

Katie picked one up. A long, vinelike string was knotted to the stick at one end. The other end of the string had been tied into a loop.

"What are these for?" Kevin asked Mr. G.

"Good question," Mr. G. said. "They're for fun."

Katie stared at her stick. It didn't look like much fun.

"It's a game," Mr. G. explained. "You toss the ring end of the rope in the air and try to catch it with the stick."

One by one the kids tried the game. Katie tossed the ringed end of the rope up, and then aimed the stick underneath. *Oops. Not even close.*

"This is hard," Kadeem said as he tossed his ringed rope.

"I did it!" Emma S. shouted excitedly.

"Me too!" Andy Epstein cheered.

"Me three!" Mandy announced to the class.

"Almost," Emma W. said. She tossed her rope in the air again for another try.

Katie didn't say anything. She was too busy focusing on catching the rope ring. She tossed it up, aimed her stick, and . . .

"I got it!" she shouted. "Huzzah!"

Mr. G. laughed. "Huzzah, indeed!" he cheered.

Tossing the rope ring up and catching it with the stick was fun. But Katie still didn't understand one thing.

"What does this game have to do with Thanksgiving, Mr. G.?" she asked.

"The game is called hoop stick," Mr. G. explained. "And it was a game Wampanoag children used to play. It taught them important skills."

"What's so important about catching a string with a stick?" Kevin asked.

"It helps develop hand-eye coordination," Mr. G. said. "That was important to the Wampanoags. They used bows and arrows when they were hunting their food. They needed to have good aim."

Katie frowned. She was sure glad they were catching string instead of hunting. She could never imagine hunting. But she figured the Wampanoags had to hunt to live. They probably didn't have tofurkey back then.

"This is the kind of lesson I like," Kevin said.

"Me too," Emma W. said. She tossed her ring up in the air. "Did it!" she cheered.

"I wouldn't even mind doing hoop stick homework," Kadeem said. "I wish I was a Wampanoag kid."

Katie gulped. Kadeem had just made a wish. That was *soooo* not good.

"You do not!" Katie shouted at Kadeem. "You do not wish anything!"

Everyone stopped tossing and catching, and stared right at Katie.

"What's up with *you*, Katie Kazoo?" Kadeem asked her.

Katie didn't know what to say. She knew wishes could be bad things. She also knew she couldn't tell her friends why. They wouldn't believe her, even if she did.

★ ★ ★

It had all started back in third grade on one terrible, horrible, miserable day. First, Katie had missed catching the football and lost a game for her team. Then she'd fallen in the mud and ruined her brand-new, favorite jeans. And then she'd stood up in front of the whole class, and let out the biggest, loudest burp in the history of Cherrydale Elementary School. *A real record breaker*. Talk about embarrassing.

That night, Katie had wished that she could be anyone but herself. There must have been a shooting star overhead when Katie made her wish because the next day the magic wind arrived.

The magic wind was a wild, powerful tornado that blew only around Katie. It was so strong that it was able to blow her right out of her own body, and into someone else's. One . . . two . . . switcheroo!

The first time the magic wind came, it turned her into Speedy, the class hamster. Katie spent the whole morning stuck in a cage, going around and around on a hamster wheel and eating wooden chew sticks. Those sticks tasted awful—even worse than the food in the school cafeteria!

Katie was really glad when the magic wind returned later that day and changed her back into herself. Unfortunately, that wasn't the end of the magic wind and its switcheroos. The wind came back again and again. Sometimes it turned her into animals, sometimes into grown-ups, and sometimes into other kids, like Emma W. or Kevin.

The time Katie had turned into Kevin had been especially bad. The magic wind came right in the middle of his karate tournament. Katie tried to break a board with her foot, and fell on her rear end, in front of the whole audience. That had been *really* embarrassing—especially for Kevin.

Another time, the magic wind switcherooed Katie into Louie, the owner of the pizzeria at the Cherrydale Mall. Katie didn't know *anything* about making pizza. What a mess that had been!

And then there was the time the wind came and switcherooed Katie into her favorite author, Nellie Farrow. It happened right before Nellie was supposed to talk to the fourth grade about her new book. The trouble was, Katie hadn't read the book yet. Because of Katie, Nellie had looked like a fool in front of her fans!

As far as Katie was concerned, wishes caused

nothing but trouble. But of course she couldn't tell her friends that. Still, she had to say something. Everyone in the class was staring at her.

"Look, Kadeem," Katie told him finally. "Being a Wampanoag in Pilgrim times wasn't all fun. They had to hunt for their own food and sew their own clothes. It wasn't like they had a mall nearby where they could buy everything."

"That's very true, Katie," Mr. G. told her. "The Wampanoag Indians didn't have it easy. Neither did the Pilgrims. In fact, you guys are going to find out just what life was like back then."

"We are?" Andy asked. "How?"

"We're going on a very special field trip," Mr. G. said.

"Back in time?" Mandy asked.

The kids all laughed. But Mr. G. didn't. "Sort of," he told Mandy. "It will *feel* like we've gone back in time. On Thursday, we're going to visit the Good Morrow Village."

"What's that?" Kadeem asked.

"The Good Morrow Village is a living museum," Mr. G. explained. "It's a pretend village from the year 1627. It looks a lot like Plymouth looked when the Pilgrims and Wampanoags had the first Thanksgiving. The village is filled with actors playing the Pilgrims and the Native Americans. They're going to show us what life was like in 1627."

"Why is it called Good Morrow?" Katie asked Mr. G.

"Because *good morrow* is how the Pilgrims said hello," her teacher explained. "And these people will be welcoming us to a time and place very different than how we live today."

Wow! Katie was very excited. This could possibly be the very best field trip ever! It was too bad she had to wait until Thursday to go.

Not that Katie was *wishing* the field trip was tomorrow or anything. She knew better than to do that!

Chapter 3

"I don't know what I'm most thankful for," Katie's best friend Suzanne Lock said as the fourth-graders left school at the end of the day. She pulled a mirror out of her backpack. "I'm thankful for how big my eyes are, and how curly my hair is. And of course I have a really great smile. It's so hard to choose."

Katie sighed. Suzanne was definitely missing the point of Thanksgiving time.

"I'm thankful for all the fun things that happen this time of year," Katie said. "Like the town bonfire."

"I think it's so nice that the whole town gets together the night before the Thanksgiving Day football game," Emma W. agreed. "Lacey says the town bonfire really gets the team psyched up."

Katie nodded. Lacey would know. Emma W.'s big sister was in high school and friendly with guys on the football team.

"I love the corn on the cob that they cook on the bonfire," Kevin said.

Suzanne gave him a funny look. "I thought you liked tomatoes," she said.

Kevin smiled. "A guy can't live on just tomatoes."

Katie said, "I bet the Wampanoags ate a lot of corn."

"We're going to find out," Emma W. said. "I'm really thankful for that field trip. It sounds amazing."

"Maybe we should call the holiday *Fanks*giving," Kadeem joked.

"Why would we call it that?" Katie asked him.

"Because everything we're thankful for starts with F," he explained. "Fire, food, football, and field trips."

"Don't forget family," Katie pointed out.

"And friends," Emma W. added.

"Well, I'm thankful for my new dress," Suzanne said. "That doesn't begin with an *F*. My mom bought it for me to wear to Thanksgiving dinner at my grandma's house. Did I tell you about it? It's got fall colors in it. Orange, red, yellow, and brown. And the sleeves are . . ."

"Um . . . I gotta run," Kevin said. "I don't want to be late for karate practice."

"I'll leave with you," Emma W. said. "I have to help my mom take care of my brothers."

"Hey, wait for me," Kadeem added. "I have to . . . well . . . I just have to go!"

Katie sighed. The other kids were really just in a rush to get away from Suzanne. None of them cared a lot about what her new Thanksgiving dress looked like.

Katie didn't really care about the dress, either. But even Suzanne's bragging couldn't put her in a bad mood today. She had so many things making her happy. There was no better place to be on Thanksgiving than Cherrydale!

★ ★ ★

"Mom!" Katie shouted as she ran into the house later that afternoon. "I have amazing news!"

Aroo! Ruff! Katie's dog, Pepper, came running as soon as he heard Katie's voice.

Katie bent down and scratched her chocolate and white cocker spaniel under his chin. "Don't worry," she told him. "You'll get to hear the exciting news, I promise."

Katie's mom hurried out of the kitchen to greet her. "Hi there, Kit Kat," she said. "I've got something exciting to tell you, too."

Katie smiled broadly. Wow! Two surprises in one day! How awesome was that?

"You go first," Katie's mother told her.

"Okay," Katie said excitedly. "I just found out that on Thursday, we're going on the most amazing field trip ever! We're visiting a Pilgrim village. Well, not a real one. That would be impossible. But a village that's just like one the Pilgrims lived in. The whole fourth grade is going."

"Wow!" Mrs. Carew exclaimed. "That *is* exciting. Isn't it, Pepper?"

Aruff! Pepper barked happily at the sound of his name.

"Now, what's your surprise?" Katie asked her mom.

Mrs. Carew smiled. "We're going to New York City!"

"To see cousin Emily?" Katie asked excitedly. Emily was her favorite cousin.

"Yep," her mom replied. "And Aunt Alison and Uncle Charlie, of course."

Katie giggled. Emily was only a teenager. *Of course* she still lived with her parents.

"We're going to be leaving a week from Wednesday, right after school," Katie's mom said. "It's all set. I just finished making the arrangements."

Katie stopped smiling. Had she heard her

mom right? "Next *Wednesday*?" she asked nervously.

"Yep," Katie's mother replied.

"But that's the day before Thanksgiving," Katie told her mom. "We can't go then. If we do, I'll miss the bonfire. And if we're in New York, I won't get to go to the high-school Thanksgiving Day football game."

"No, I guess not," Katie's mom said. "Thanksgiving here is wonderful. But this year we'll be doing something different. It's going to be great."

Katie frowned. She couldn't believe her mother thought that going to New York for Thanksgiving was going to be great. Katie certainly didn't think so. She thought it was going to be rotten.

Suddenly, she didn't feel very thankful anymore.

Chapter 4

"You know, Jeremy, you're not the only one who's feeling bad around here," Suzanne said as she plopped her tray across the table from Katie and Jeremy.

Katie looked at Suzanne with amazement. Had she really noticed that Katie was unhappy, too? Wow! That was very un-Suzanne of her.

"*I'm* absolutely miserable!" Suzanne told the kids.

Katie sighed. Never mind. Suzanne was still Suzanne.

"Why are *you* unhappy?" Emma W. asked Suzanne.

"Because my mother is making me wear last year's overalls to the corn shucking," Suzanne told her.

"So what?" Jeremy asked her. "You get all messy at a corn shucking."

"You really do," Emma W. said. "Last year I had corn silk in my hair when I got home."

"That's nothing," Kadeem said. "I had it in my underwear. And I have no idea how it got there."

The kids all giggled. All except Katie, that is. Just hearing the kids talking about shucking all the corn for the bonfire made her even sadder.

"That's because you, Kevin, and George were making it rain corn silk all over the place while we did the work," Suzanne reminded Kadeem.

"We still shucked plenty of corn," Kevin said. "We just had fun while we did it."

"It's not like *you* worked hard, Suzanne," Jeremy reminded her. "I remember you spent the whole time talking about your hair."

“I’ll bet you this year I shuck more corn than you do,” Suzanne said.

“I doubt it,” Kevin told her. “Don’t forget Jeremy is an athlete.”

“He plays soccer,” Suzanne reminded him. “What’s he going to do? Shuck corn with his feet?”

“He’s also a boy,” Kevin said.

“So what? Girls can do anything boys can!” Suzanne exclaimed. “And better. We’ll prove it. This year, I think we should have a contest. The girls against the boys. To see who can shuck the most corn.”

“Oh please, don’t make me laugh,” Kadeem said.

“We’re not laughing,” Mandy butted in.

“Not one bit,” Emma W. agreed.

“Then you’re on!” Jeremy exclaimed. “Boys against girls.”

“We’re going to beat you,” Suzanne told Jeremy. “Aren’t we, Katie?”

Katie didn’t know what to say. She hated

when she was caught in the middle between her two best friends.

"I'm not going to the corn shucking," Katie told Suzanne quietly.

"What do you mean?" Suzanne asked. "We always go to the corn shucking together."

"Not this year," Katie said. "I can't go to the bonfire or the football game. We're going to New York for Thanksgiving."

"When are you leaving?" Suzanne asked.

"Next Wednesday, right after school," Katie told her.

"But we shuck the corn on *Tuesday* night," Suzanne said. "You'll still be here then."

"Yeah," Katie agreed. "But I . . ."

"Come on, Katie. We need your help," Suzanne said. "We need all the girls we can get if we're going to beat the boys."

"Please help us, Katie," Emma W. said. "We don't want to have to listen to the boys bragging all the way until next Thanksgiving."

"And if they win, you know that's what

they'll do," Suzanne said. She shook her head angrily. "I really hate when people brag."

That made Katie laugh. No one bragged more than Suzanne.

"Okay," Katie said finally. "Count me in."

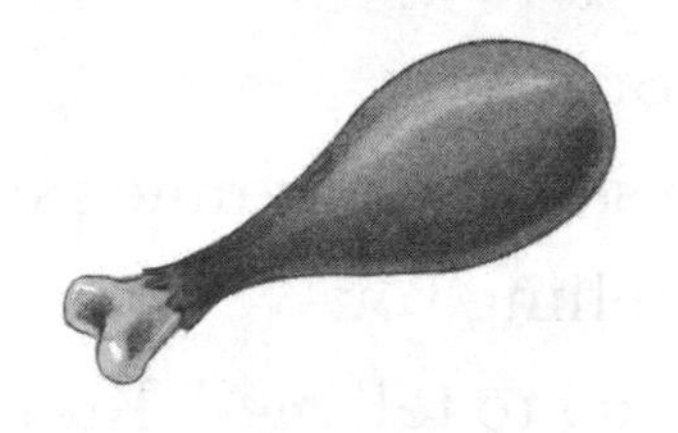

Chapter 5

"Hey, Katie, do you want to come over and kick around a soccer ball?" Jeremy asked after school that afternoon.

Katie opened her mouth to say "sure." But before she could squeak out a sound, Suzanne grabbed her and pulled her by the elbow.

"Katie can't go with you today," Suzanne told Jeremy. "We're having a team practice."

"What team?" Katie and Jeremy asked at the exact same time.

"The *girls'* team," Suzanne said. "We're going to have to practice a lot if we're going to beat you boys at shucking corn."

"How do you practice shucking corn?" Jeremy asked Suzanne.

"It's a team secret," Suzanne said. "I'm definitely not telling you."

"Are you going to tell *me*?" Katie asked.

"As soon as we get to my house," Suzanne assured her. "Now come on. We *girls* are all waiting for you."

Katie didn't know what to say. She wanted to go play soccer with Jeremy. But she had promised to be on the girls' corn-shucking team. And a promise was a promise.

"Sorry, Jeremy," Katie apologized. "Maybe we can play soccer tomorrow."

"We're probably having team practice then, too," Suzanne told Katie. "So I wouldn't make any plans."

Katie was not happy as she walked off with Suzanne. She really hated being caught in the middle between her two best friends. But once again, that was exactly where she was.

"What's with all the baby dolls?" Zoe Canter asked as the girls followed Suzanne into her room later that afternoon.

Suzanne was carrying a huge pile of her baby sister Heather's dolls in her arms.

"Husking is kind of like undressing corn," Suzanne explained as she plopped the dolls onto the floor. "So we're going to practice undressing these dolls until we can do it really fast."

"That's stupid," Mandy said. "There aren't any snaps or zippers on corn husks."

"True," Miriam Chan agreed. "And corn doesn't have arms or legs, either."

"Corn only has ears," Emma W. said. "Get it? *Ears* of corn?"

Katie laughed. Emma W. really did know some funny jokes. "Good one, Emma," she said.

"Thanks," Emma W. answered. She looked down at the pile of dolls. "Are you sure Heather isn't going to be upset that we're

using her dolls for our practice?" she asked Suzanne. "My little brothers get really mad when anyone plays with one of their toys."

"Heather won't care," Suzanne said. "She's got lots of toys. And besides, she's a girl. So she would probably *want* us to use her dolls so our team can win."

Katie wasn't so sure about that. Suzanne's baby sister wasn't even two years old yet. She doubted she understood about girls' teams and boys' teams.

Still, Suzanne was now the team captain—although no one was really sure how that had happened. They hadn't taken a vote or anything. She'd just sort of taken over. And, as team captain, Suzanne was in charge.

"Okay, everybody, grab a baby doll," Suzanne said. "And when I say go, you start undressing it."

"Aren't you going to practice, too?" Emma S. asked Suzanne.

"No," Suzanne said. "Somebody has to watch the clock to see how long it takes."

"How come *you* get to be the clock watcher?" Becky Stern asked her.

"Because it's my room and my clock," Suzanne said. "And I'm the captain. You don't argue with the captain."

Becky sighed, but she didn't say anything. What would be the point?

"Okay," Suzanne said. "On your marks. Get set. Go!"

Katie started to unsnap the little pink snowsuit her baby doll was wearing. It wasn't easy. There were tiny snaps, and the doll's arms and legs didn't move very well.

She was so focused on undressing her doll that Katie didn't notice Heather toddling into the room. None of the girls did—until she let out a really loud scream.

"Mine!" Heather shrieked.

The girls all looked up.

Heather walked over to Miriam and

grabbed the doll out of her hand. "Mine!" she shouted again.

"Heather, get out of here," Suzanne said. "This is *my* playdate."

But Heather didn't leave. Instead, she walked over to Zoe.

"Mine!" Heather shouted again. She pulled so hard on the doll's feet that one of the legs broke off. "Waaahhhhh!" she cried out. "Dolly broke!"

"Now look what you've done," Suzanne shouted at Heather.

"Waaaahhhhhh!" Heather cried even louder.

Mrs. Lock came running into the room. "What's going on in here?" she asked Suzanne.

"Heather is ruining our team practice," Suzanne told her mother.

"Why do you have all her dolls?" Mrs. Lock asked.

"We need them to get used to undressing corn," Suzanne explained.

Mrs. Lock stared at the pile of doll clothes

on Suzanne's floor. She listened to Heather wailing. Then she took the broken doll from Zoe's hands.

"Practice is over," Mrs. Lock told Suzanne. "Clean up this mess, and put the dolls back in Heather's room."

Mrs. Lock bent down and scooped Heather up in her arms. Then she popped the doll's leg back where it belonged, and handed it to Heather.

"Now your doll's all better," Mrs. Lock said.

Suzanne's little sister stopped crying immediately.

Suzanne looked down at the mess on her floor. It was going to take a long time to clean everything up. "My mom always takes Heather's side," she muttered under her breath. But she started picking up the doll clothes, anyway.

Apparently, in Suzanne's house, her *mom* was the captain. And like Suzanne said, you don't argue with the captain.

Chapter 6

"I am not going to cut my nails," Suzanne shouted at Jeremy as they stood outside school on Thursday morning. The fourth grade was waiting for the field trip bus to arrive.

"You have to," Jeremy said. "Having long nails makes it easier for you to open the corn husk and pull it off."

"It does not," Suzanne said.

"Yes it does," Jeremy insisted.

"Then why don't you grow *your* nails longer," Suzanne demanded.

"I don't have time to grow my nails by next Tuesday," Jeremy said. "And besides, I'm a boy. Boys don't have long nails."

"Your loss," Suzanne said. She flipped her hair over her shoulder and turned her back on Jeremy.

Katie frowned. She was really sick of her best friends fighting. They'd been at it the entire week—ever since their bet. Apparently, even though it wasn't okay for the teammates to argue with their captains, it was just fine for captains to argue with each other.

But that didn't mean Katie had to listen. The minute the first bus arrived, she hurried on and made sure she got a seat next to Emma W. Mandy and Miriam were across the aisle.

"I can't wait until we get to the Good Morrow Village," Katie told Emma W. "I heard you get to see people making candles."

Emma W. said, "Lacey went to this place when she was in fourth grade. She said she got to do some weaving. And she told me not to miss the glassblowing."

"Glassblowing?" Katie asked. "What's that?"

"It's when someone uses a pipe to blow air

into melted glass," Emma W. said. "It's how they used to make bowls and vases and stuff back then."

"Are you girls practicing your finger exercises?" Suzanne shouted from her seat three rows back. She began moving her pointer fingers up and down, and in and out.

"It would be nice if Suzanne would stop exercising her *tongue*," Mandy whispered across the aisle to Katie and Emma W. "I am so sick of hearing about this corn-shucking contest."

"What else did Lacey say we should see at the village?" Katie asked Emma W., trying to change the subject back to the field trip.

"She said to make sure we visit the Wampanoag village," Emma W. told her. "Some of the kids in her grade actually got to help hollow out a log to build a canoe."

"That sounds really cool," Kevin said.

"I know," Emma W. said. "Maybe we'll even get to go canoeing while we're there."

Jeremy heard them talking. "I think they should send Suzanne off in a canoe," he said. "Up a creek without a paddle."

The boys all laughed.

"I heard that! You just want me gone because then you'll win the contest," Suzanne told Jeremy.

“That’s not it,” Jeremy said. “I’m just sick of hearing your voice.”

Katie wanted to plug her ears. Everything about this Thanksgiving was turning out all wrong! The only thing she’d been looking forward to was this field trip. And if Suzanne and Jeremy didn’t stop their fighting, that was going to be ruined, too.

Chapter 7

"Prithee be careful," a woman in a long gray dress and white bonnet said as Katie walked along a muddy path at the Good Morrow Village. "We have had much rainfall as of late and the road is slippery."

Katie looked at the woman and smiled. She loved her voice. It sounded almost like she had an English accent, which made sense since the Pilgrims were from England.

"By what name are you called?" the woman asked Katie.

"I'm Katie," she answered. "What's your name?"

"I am Patience Mitchell," the woman in the

gray dress said. She pointed to one of the little wooden houses just up the hill. It had a thatched roof and a white fence. There was a small flower garden in front. "That is my home."

Katie nodded and grinned. She knew that wasn't true. This woman was an actress playing the part of a Pilgrim named Patience Mitchell. It was kind of like a game all the actors played. So Katie played along with it. It made it much more fun.

"Hi, Patience," Katie said.

Just then, Kadeem came running over to Katie and Patience. "Excuse me. Where's the bathroom?" he asked Patience.

Patience looked at him curiously. "You wish to bathe?" she asked.

Kadeem shook his head. "No. I gotta *go*," he told her. "Bad."

"Oh," Patience said. "Well, we Pilgrims use chamber pots for that. But visitors may go to the gray wooden building up this hill and to the left."

"Thanks," Kadeem said as he raced up the hill as fast as he could.

Katie thought about asking what a chamber pot was. But it sounded kind of gross. So she changed the subject.

"What do you do here in the village?" she asked Patience.

"I spend a great deal of my day making cornhusk dolls for the children," Patience said. "Prithee, come visit my home. My mother will be grinding corn while I make my dolls. Perhaps you will even help us bake cornbread in our hearth."

Katie didn't know what to say. Patience was very nice. However, right now the last thing Katie wanted to think about was corn husks. So she just said, "I'll try and stop by."

"I do hope so," Patience said. She gave Katie a small curtsy. "And now I must return to my home. Pray, remember me."

Katie watched curiously as Patience walked off. Pray, remember me. What a strange way to say good-bye.

"Katie, wait up!"

Katie saw Emma W. and Mandy walking toward her.

"What do you want to see first?" Katie asked the girls.

"I'm not sure," Emma W. said. "There are so many places to go."

"Mr. G. said we could go wherever we wanted, as long as we all met for lunch at 12:30," Katie said. "We don't have to stick together as a grade."

"I just want to be someplace where Suzanne can't find us," Mandy told Emma W. and Katie.

"We could go to one of the houses and watch a Pilgrim woman do some embroidery," Emma W. said. "Or maybe visit the place where they make horseshoes."

"Or maybe instead of starting at the Pilgrim houses, we could visit the Wampanoags first," Katie suggested.

"That does sound cool," Mandy agreed. "Okay. Let's go there first."

★ ★ ★

The Wampanoag village looked very different from the Pilgrim town. While the Pilgrim town was full of little wooden houses with small gardens, the Native American homes looked more like round huts made of tree bark and woven mats.

"Welcome to our *wetu*," a Native American woman in a beautiful, brown suede dress said as she greeted Katie, Emma W., and Mandy a few minutes later.

"Your what?" Emma W. asked. "I'm sorry. I don't speak Wampanoag."

The woman smiled. "*Wetu* is our word for home," she explained. "And I am very glad to have visitors. Please, *noe winyah*."

"No what?" Mandy asked.

"*Noe winyah*," the woman answered. "It means *come in*."

"Thank you," Katie said as she and her friends stepped inside.

Can I offer you some *sobaheg*?"

"I'm not sure," Katie admitted. "What is *sobaheg*?"

"A meat and vegetable stew," the woman replied. "It's very delicious."

"No, thank you," Katie said. "I am a vegetarian."

"What is that?" the woman asked.

Katie had a feeling that in real life the woman knew what a vegetarian was. But a Wampanoag woman in the 1600s probably wouldn't. "I don't eat meat," Katie explained.

"But *I* do," Mandy said. "And I am starving."

As the Wampanoag woman gave Mandy a heaping helping of *sobaheg*, Katie looked around the *wetu*. There were beautiful woven mats on the floors. And although she didn't like the fur skins that seemed to be everywhere, Katie understood that back in the 1600s, when there was no heat other than a fire, furs were probably needed for the Wampanoags to keep warm.

"I love this basket," Katie said, pointing to a white woven basket with a flowery design on top.

"Thank you," the Wampanoag woman said. "I wove that myself, from porcupine quills."

"*Real* porcupine quills?" Mandy asked. "Aren't they really sharp?"

The woman laughed. "Very sharp. But they are also very beautiful."

Mandy and Emma W. took two last bites of their stew, and then stood up to leave. "Thank you for the stew. It was yummy," Emma W. said. "I've never tasted anything like that before."

"You have never visited a Wampanoag village before," the Native American woman reminded her. "But I hope you will come back."

"I hope so, too," Emma W. told her. "I want to bring my whole family here." Then she stopped for a minute. "Well, maybe just my older sister and my brother who is in first grade. I have twin brothers who are only two, and they'd probably turn your whole house upside down. They are wild."

The Wampanoag woman smiled. "Not as wild as the many wild animals in our forest."

"You don't know my brothers," Emma W. reminded her.

Katie laughed. Emma W. wasn't kidding. Her twin brothers were definitely a handful.

"Come on, you guys," Mandy urged. "We haven't been to any of the Pilgrim houses yet. I want to see them, too."

★ ★ ★

A few minutes later, Katie, Emma W., and Mandy found themselves in a completely different world from the Wampanoag village. Instead of wearing animal skins and brightly colored jewelry like the Native Americans, the Pilgrims were all dressed in the same colors—gray, black, navy blue, and white. There were no cars, of course. Or sidewalks. And every house was tiny. It was so different from Cherrydale and Katie's daily life . . . Then she heard Suzanne shouting at Jeremy. *That* was very familiar.

"I was at the front of the line before you," Suzanne shouted from outside the candlemaker's home.

"You were, but then you got out of line," Jeremy shouted back.

"I had to go to the bathroom," Suzanne told him. "Now I'm back."

"Exactly," Jeremy answered. "So go to the *back* of this line!"

Katie sighed. No matter where she wound up, or what year it was, some things in her life never changed. It was embarrassing to hear Suzanne and Jeremy arguing like that. It wasn't like the fourth-graders from Cherrydale Elementary were the only visitors to the Good Morrow Village. What if other people thought all the kids from their school were as badly behaved as her two best friends? That would be awful!

"Let's get out of here," Katie told Emma W. and Mandy.

"Right behind you," Emma W. agreed.

"Good-bye, twenty-first century!" Mandy added.

Chapter 8

"And now we leave the wax to cool," the candlemaker said as she placed several candle molds near a window. "Thanks to the candles, we will have light in the darkness. Huzzah!"

Katie almost laughed. It seemed a little weird for someone to be so excited about candle wax. But then again, everything about the Pilgrim village was a little weird.

When the girls left the candle-making house, Mandy pointed to another small wooden house and said, "I wonder what's going on there."

"Oh, that's Patience Mitchell's house," Katie said. "She makes dolls."

Mandy and Emma W. wanted to go see how that was done.

"Good morrow, Katie," Patience greeted her. "I am so glad to have visitors."

"This is Emma, and this is Mandy," Katie said, introducing her friends.

"Good morrow to you both," Patience said. "My mother is grinding corn into flour today. Corn is very important. Our Wampanoag neighbors taught us how to plant and grow it. Perhaps later, you girls will try to make your way through our village corn maze. But here is a warning: The stalks are high and the paths are twisty."

"Katie said you make dolls with corn husks," Emma W. told Patience. "I'd like to see how you do that. We always have a big bonfire in our town on Wednesday night, right before Thanksgiving. We serve corn to the whole town. There will be plenty of corn husks."

Katie frowned. She'd been having such a good time that she'd almost forgotten that she wouldn't be around for the bonfire. *Until now*.

"This is one of my dolls," Patience told the girls. She held up a little figure made of dried corn husks and string. It kind of looked like a man.

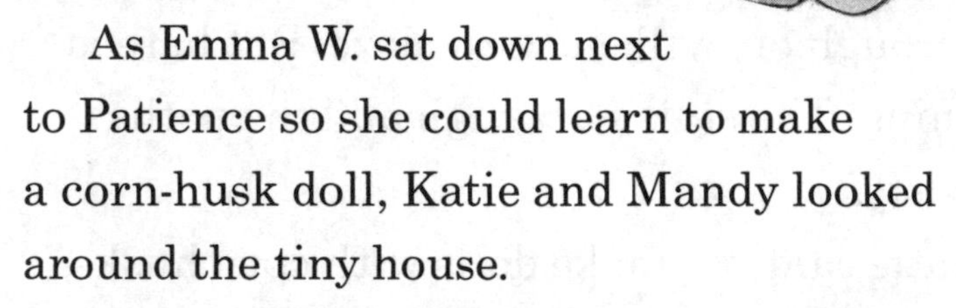

"Is it hard to make a doll like that?" Emma W. asked her.

"Not at all," Patience answered. "Prithee, sit here beside me."

As Emma W. sat down next to Patience so she could learn to make a corn-husk doll, Katie and Mandy looked around the tiny house.

"Those dolls are scary-looking," Katie whispered to Mandy. "I think Suzanne's little sister would cry if she got one of those as a present."

"Nah, she wouldn't be scared of a doll," Mandy whispered back. "Nothing's scarier than having Suzanne as a big sister."

Katie laughed and then glanced over to where Patience and Emma W. were sitting. Patience was helping Emma W. tie four corn husks together. She showed her how to trim the edges and fold down the husks to form the doll's head. Emma W. was watching Patience's hands. But Patience seemed to be looking at Katie, not Emma W. And Katie wasn't sure, but she thought Patience might be giving her a funny look.

Oh no! Had Patience heard what Katie had said about the dolls? She hadn't meant to

hurt Patience's feelings. Before Katie could apologize to Patience, Kevin and Kadeem wandered into the house.

"We've been looking for you. It's almost lunchtime," Kevin told Katie and Mandy.

"Oh, are you children going to the groaning board?" Patience asked the boys.

"The *what*?" Kadeem asked. He shook his head slightly. "I don't understand anything anyone says around this place."

"The groaning board," Patience repeated. "It's a big feast."

"It's not meat stew, is it?" Katie asked Patience. "Because that's all they had at the Wampanoag village, and I don't eat meat."

Patience smiled at Katie. "There will be many vegetables and fruits at the groaning board," she assured her.

"Great," Katie said. "I'm starving."

"Me too," Emma W. said. "I just want to finish my doll."

Five minutes later, she put her doll in her

knapsack and smiled at Patience. "Thank you for teaching me how to do this. I'm going to make a lot of these with the corn we husk next Tuesday night."

"I'm glad to have helped," Patience said. "Fare thee well. Enjoy the meal."

Emma W., Mandy, and Katie headed off after Kevin and Kadeem. As she walked, Katie heard her stomach rumble. She also felt a little chilly.

"Oh no!" Katie exclaimed. "I left my jacket back at Patience's house. I have to run back and get it."

"I'll save you a seat at the table," Emma W. told her.

"Thanks," Katie said. "I'll be really quick."

Katie wasn't far from Patience's house when she suddenly felt a cool breeze blowing against the back of her neck. It was really getting cold out. She really did need her jacket. But before Katie could reach the house, the gentle breeze began to pick up speed. Katie looked around. That was weird. The leaves on the trees weren't moving at all. In fact, the wind didn't seem to be blowing anywhere but around Katie.

Uh-oh. That could only mean one thing. This was no ordinary wind. This was *the magic wind*!

"Oh no!" Katie shouted. "Not now. Not before I get to eat at the groaning board! I'm starving!"

But the magic wind didn't care that Katie was hungry. And it didn't care that there was a whole feast waiting. The wind just kept blowing, circling faster and faster around Katie, whirring around her like a wild tornado. It was so powerful, she had to grab on to a nearby tree just to keep from being blown away.

Katie shut her eyes tight and tried not to cry.

And then, it stopped. Just like that. The magic wind was gone.

But so was Katie Carew. She'd turned into someone else. One . . . two . . . switcheroo!

But who?

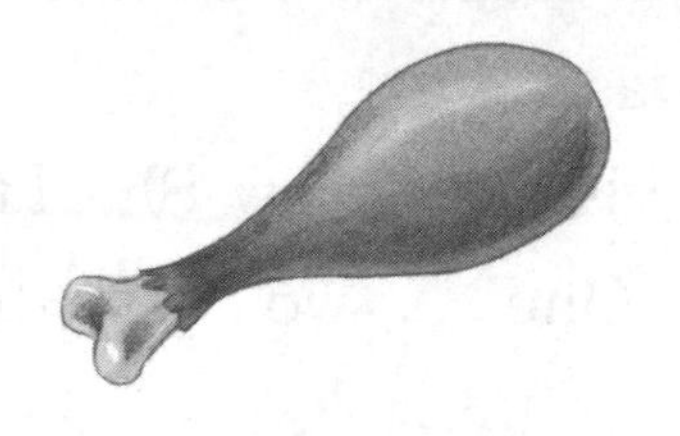

Chapter 9

Slowly, Katie opened her eyes and looked around. Everywhere she looked she could see small cottages and people dressed as Pilgrims. That meant Katie was still at the Good Morrow Village.

Okay, so now Katie knew *where* she was. But she still didn't know *who* she was. She looked down at her feet. She could barely see them under the long petticoats that were beneath her skirt. But from what she could tell, her way-cool, red high-top sneakers were gone. Instead, Katie was wearing a pair of stiff, hard, leather boots.

The boots weren't very comfortable. But

then again, neither were the itchy wool stockings she had on. And her long skirt and thick petticoats were heavy and hot.

Wait a minute. Katie didn't wear long skirts and petticoats. She didn't wear wool stockings, either. No fourth-grade girls did. Not even Suzanne. And *she* wore a lot of really crazy things.

The only people Katie had seen wearing petticoats were the Pilgrim women at the Good Morrow Village.

That had to mean that Katie was now one of the Pilgrims. But which one? And what was she supposed to be doing?

"Prithee, Patience," Katie heard a woman say. "These young ladies would like to see a doll being made."

Katie turned around, hoping to see Patience, since Patience might know what Katie was supposed to be doing.

But Patience wasn't anywhere around. The only people Katie saw were the woman who played Patience's mother, and three girls in jeans and sweatshirts.

"Patience?" the actress playing the Pilgrim mother repeated.

Katie looked around again. The three girls and the Pilgrim woman were all staring right at her.

Uh-oh! That could only mean one thing. The magic wind had switcherooed Katie into Patience Mitchell. And right now, those girls were waiting to see Patience make her corn-husk dolls. But Katie had no idea how to make dolls or anything else out of corn husks. She hadn't watched what Emma W. had been doing. This was *soooo* not good.

"Patience, prithee, make a doll," the actress playing Patience's mom said again. She had said prithee, but this time her voice was a lot more stern.

Katie looked down at the huge pile of corn husks by her feet. Then she looked at the dolls Patience had lined up on a shelf behind her.

They didn't look so hard to make. They were really just some string tied around husks to form a head, a waist, and some arms and legs. Katie knew how to tie knots. Maybe this wouldn't be so hard, after all.

Katie picked up four husks and a small piece of string. She looked at the three girls. "Okay, you guys, so first I tie a piece of string here," she said, tying some string where she thought the doll's neck would be.

"Hey!" one of the girls said. "How come you're not talking like the other Pilgrims here?"

Oops. Katie had forgotten about the Pilgrim-speak thing. She wasn't supposed to sound like a fourth-grade girl from Cherrydale. At least not as long as she was still Patience Mitchell.

"I mean, *prithee,* watch while I tie the string around the doll's neck," Katie corrected herself.

But the corn husks weren't easy to hold together. And the string was small and hard to tie. It kept slipping from her hands.

"Um, have you ever done this before?" one of the kids said.

"This is kind of boring, anyway. Let's leave," one of the other girls whispered to her friends, loud enough for Katie to hear.

Katie frowned. She was trying her best. Why couldn't these kids give her a break?

As soon as the girls left the cottage, the woman playing Patience's mother said, "What is the matter with you?"

Katie scratched at her legs. The wool stockings she was wearing made her itch.

And she was starting to feel really uncomfortable. Who wouldn't? Under her thick waistcoat, Katie was wearing a long-sleeved blouse and a very thick, tight stay. The stay was like an undershirt, except it was really, really stiff and uncomfortable. It felt like there was a wooden board sewn into it or something.

Katie was tired of being a Pilgrim doll maker. She needed a break.

"Patience, why are you not working?" the woman asked her.

Katie didn't know what to say. She couldn't tell the woman that she had to get out of there before any more kids came and wanted her to make another doll. But she did have to get out of there.

"I . . . um . . . I have to use the change pot," Katie said finally.

"The what?" the woman asked.

"The change pot," Katie repeated. "You know, I have to *go*."

"Oh, the *chamber* pot," Patience's mother corrected her.

Katie frowned. This Pilgrim-speak was hard.

"Well, go then," the woman said. "And pray, be fast. We shall have more visitors within the hour."

"Yes, ma'am," Katie said. She ran out the door.

"Aren't you going to say 'Pray, remember

me?'" Patience's mother called after her.

But Katie was already out of there.

Chapter 10

"Boy, it's hot out," Katie murmured to herself as she stepped out of the cottage. It was November, and the air was actually kind of cool, but with all the layers of clothing she was wearing, it felt like summer. She rolled up her sleeves of her waistcoat, and looked around for the nearest bathroom.

A moment later, a man dressed as a Pilgrim farmer came racing over to her. "Modesty," he hissed in her ear. "Roll those sleeves back down."

"Oh, sorry," Katie apologized. "I . . . uh . . . I forgot I wasn't supposed to roll up my sleeves. I was just going on my break."

“Mind the accent,” the farmer whispered.

Oops. Katie had forgotten to sound like a Pilgrim.

“Righty-o,” Katie said. It was what an English kid on a TV show she liked to watch was always saying.

The man looked at her strangely.

Uh-oh. Apparently the Pilgrims didn’t say things like *righty-o*, either.

“I guess I’m getting a bit dizzy. I think it’s the heat and . . .” Katie’s stomach rumbled. “I’m a little hungry, too.”

“Then prithee, go to the groaning board for some food,” the farmer told her. “And then back to work.”

The groaning board was set up in a restaurant that was designed to look like a Pilgrim home. Katie had never seen so much food in her life.

Some of it looked delicious. There were salad and fixings, and cooked vegetables. The

rolls were huge. But there was also some sort of boiled meat. That looked really gross. Katie walked right past it and began piling veggies onto a plate. Then she grabbed a knife and fork and looked around the room for a seat. Oh cool. There was a space right near Kevin, Andy, and Mandy.

"Hi," Katie said. "Mind if I sit here?"

Kevin moved over to make space for her.

"Aren't you supposed to say *Good Morrow*?" Andy asked.

Oops. "Oh, yes, of course," Katie said quickly. "I was just trying to speak the language of our visitors. Much like the Wampanoag people will try to learn English. At least, I think they will. Someday. Maybe. I'm not really sure." She turned to Kevin. "Did the Wampanoags try to learn English?"

The kids all looked at Katie strangely. But that wasn't nearly as awful as the look she was getting from the Pilgrim man standing nearby. He looked kind of mad.

hat at the candlemaker's house."

"Patience!" the Pilgrim man continued in a stern, angry voice. "I need thee to come outside. Now."

Uh-oh. That did not sound good. But Katie didn't argue. She just stood up and followed him outside to the back of the groaning board.

"Patience, what is wrong?" the Pilgrim man demanded.

Katie looked at him strangely. "Nothing."

"Pilgrims don't eat with silverware. They us their hands," he said.

"That's gross," Katie said. She covered her mouth with her hand. But it was too late. The words had already escaped.

"That's it!" the Pilgrim whispered angrily, making sure no visitors were around. "Be gon And do not return to Good Morrow Village."

"But . . ." Katie began.

"No buts," the Pilgrim man told her. And with that he walked away, leaving Katie standing all alone.

But then again, maybe he wasn't mad. Pilgrim men always looked angry. Katie had never seen a single picture of one smiling.

"This place is so cool," Kevin said as he stuffed a giant tomato into his mouth. "I really liked the crafts. I'm thinking of becoming a joiner one day."

"What would you join? A crafts club?" Katie said in surprise. "You hate that sort of thing."

The kids all stared at her again.

"How do you know that?" Kevin asked her.

Oops, again. "I . . . um . . . I mean, you don't look like someone who is a joiner," Katie corrected herself. "You look like someone who likes to do things on his own."

"I meant a furniture maker," Kevin explained to Katie. "The guy who was making his own wooden chairs without using any nails. Don't you Pilgrims call them *joiners*?"

Katie had no idea. But it sounded good. She nodded slowly and reached for her

glass of water. But the stiff stays in the
clothes made it tough for her to reach.

Oops, again and again! Katie knocke
Mandy's water glass over.

"Oh no!" Mandy shouted, jumping up
keep from getting wet.

"Excuse me," Katie apologized.

The angry Pilgrim man raced over to
table and handed Mandy a cloth napkin.
believe Patience Mitchell doth mean to s
Pray, pardon me. Isn't that so, Patience?"

Katie nodded. "Pray, pardon me," she
repeated quietly.

"Everything about you is so arsy-vars
today, Patience," the Pilgrim man said.

Katie started to giggle as she picked u
knife and fork. *Arsy-varsy?*

"Pray, what is so funny?" the Pilgrim
demanded.

"Arsy-varsy," Katie repeated. "It sound
weird."

"It means backward," Andy said. "I lea

A tear fell down her cheek. Patience had lost her job. And it was all Katie's fault. This was *sooo* not good.

Chapter 11

"I'll bet I can get to the end of this maze before you can!"

As she left the groaning board, Katie heard a familiar voice. It belonged to Suzanne. And it was coming from the giant corn maze.

"No way, Suzanne," a second voice shouted. "I'm a lot faster than you are."

The second voice was Jeremy's. Katie rolled her eyes. Apparently her two best friends were still arguing.

"But I'm a lot smarter than you are," Suzanne said. "I'm going into the maze. I dare you to go in, too."

"I never say no to a dare," Jeremy answered.

Katie frowned. Jeremy and Suzanne weren't supposed to be in the maze at all. They were supposed to be at the groaning board eating lunch. If their teacher, Ms. Sweet, realized they were missing, they would be in big trouble. Just like Katie was going to be, as soon as Mr. G. noticed that she had disappeared.

Maybe Suzanne and Jeremy didn't realize it was lunchtime. After all, there were no clocks on the walls of the little houses in the village.

"I should tell them it's lunchtime," Katie murmured to herself. "There's no reason all three of us should be in trouble."

Katie quickly ran into the maze after her friends. And then she stopped suddenly.

Whoa! It was kind of creepy in the maze. The corn stalks were so high, they towered over Katie's head, even though at the moment she was Patience, and as tall as a grown-up. Everywhere Katie looked, she saw green corn stalks. It was hard to tell which way to turn.

How was she ever going to find Suzanne and Jeremy in this thing?

"Jeremy! Get out of my way. Stop blocking me everywhere I walk."

Katie smiled at the sound of Suzanne's voice. *That* was how. All she had to do was follow the arguing.

"*You're* blocking *me*," Jeremy shouted back.

Katie turned to her right, following the sounds of the voices. And a moment later, she was face-to-face with her two best friends.

"Hi!" she greeted them. "Boy, are you guys going to be in trouble."

Jeremy and Suzanne looked at Katie strangely. It was like they had no idea who she was. Which, of course, they didn't. After all, Katie wasn't Katie anymore. She was Patience Mitchell.

"Oh. I mean, good morrow," Katie corrected herself. "You two best get to the groaning board. Your teachers will be looking for you."

"It's lunchtime?" Jeremy asked.

Katie nodded.

"We're supposed to be with the rest of the fourth grade now," Suzanne said. "This is all your fault, Jeremy."

"*My* fault?" Jeremy shouted. "You're the one who dared me to go through this maze."

"Well, you're the one who took the dare," Suzanne said.

"It doesn't matter who started it," Katie said. "What matters is that you get to the restaurant."

"She's right," Jeremy said. "We've got to get out of here."

Suzanne nodded. "Yeah. But *how* do we get out of here?"

"I think we go to the left," Jeremy said.

"I think it's the right," Suzanne told him.

Katie sighed. "Since none of us are sure, why don't we compromise and go straight?"

But going straight didn't lead them out of the maze. In fact, it just got them more lost.

"Now what?" Suzanne asked.

"How should I know?" Jeremy replied. He started walking toward the left.

"Where are you going?" Suzanne asked.

"I'm solving this maze," Jeremy answered.

"Well, wait for me," Suzanne said.

"And me," Katie added. "I don't want to be stuck in here all alone."

Jeremy and Suzanne gave Katie funny looks. Katie frowned. That hadn't sounded like a grown-up at all. But right now, Katie didn't feel like a grown-up. She felt like a fourth-grade girl. A scared fourth-grade girl. This corn maze was creepy.

"I think if we turn to the right, we'll be almost there," Suzanne said after the three of them had walked for a while.

"Okay," Jeremy agreed. "And then we should take that turn over there."

A few minutes later, a smile broke out on Suzanne's face. "Look! There's the exit!"

"I knew I could get us through this maze," Jeremy told her.

"What do you mean *you*?" Suzanne shouted.

"Stop it!" Katie shouted suddenly.

Jeremy and Suzanne both stared at her.

"You both solved the maze," Katie said. "Together. Not everything is a contest."

"It is to her," Jeremy said.

"It is to him," Suzanne said at the exact same time.

"Well, right now, you both have to get to lunch," Katie said. "And fast."

"She's right," Jeremy said.

"See you later!" they shouted to Katie as they ran off together.

With that, they were gone. And Katie was left all alone. Suddenly, she felt a cool breeze blowing on the back of her neck. She pulled her waistcoat tighter around her.

But a waistcoat wasn't any match for this breeze. This was no ordinary wind. This was the magic wind. It was back! And it was only blowing around Katie.

The magic wind grew stronger and stronger,

circling around Katie like a wild tornado. It almost knocked her out of her boots. Katie shut her eyes tightly and tried not to cry.

And then it stopped. Just like that. The magic wind was gone. Katie Kazoo was back!

So was Patience Mitchell. And, *boy,* was she confused.

Chapter 12

"What happened?" Patience asked, rubbing her eyes for a minute. She looked over at Katie. "I remember thee. The young maid who eats no meat."

"Exactly," Katie said. She was happy Patience hadn't remembered her as the girl who didn't like her dolls.

"But why art thou here?" Patience asked.

Uh-oh. Katie wasn't exactly sure how to answer that one. "Well . . . I was . . . uh . . . looking for the groaning board," she said quickly. "I have to meet my class."

There. That was at least half the truth. Katie did have to get back to the fourth-graders.

"Oh," Patience said. She thought for a minute. "Why am *I* here?" she asked Katie.

"I think you were going through the corn maze," Katie told her.

Patience thought about that for a minute. "Oh. Now I remember. Miles James told me to be gone!"

Katie frowned. That made her really sad. After all, she'd been the one to get Patience in trouble.

"Maybe you can get your job back," she suggested to Patience.

Patience shook her head. "No. I think not."

"I'm really sorry," Katie told her.

"Thank you," Patience replied.

Suddenly, Katie's stomach rumbled. She was hungry. The rest of the kids were probably almost finished eating. And Mr. G. would be worrying about her by now.

"Can you help me find the groaning board?" she asked Patience.

"For certain," Patience told her.

★★★

The fourth-graders were already eating dessert by the time Katie and Patience arrived at the groaning board. Mr. G. came running over. The Pilgrim, Miles James, was right behind him.

"Katie, where have you been?" Mr. G. asked her.

"I . . . um . . . I got lost," Katie said. That was sort of the truth. She'd been lost in the maze for a while, anyway.

"Jeremy and I were lost, too," Suzanne said. "But we found our way out of the maze without any help."

"Well, we had a little help," Jeremy admitted. "Patience was with us in the corn maze."

Suddenly, Katie got one of her great ideas. She knew just what to say to help Patience get her job back!

"Patience helped me, too. I never would have found the groaning board without her,"

Katie told Miles James. "She's helped a lot of people today."

Miles looked from Katie to Patience, and then over to Jeremy and Suzanne.

"Patience is a wonderful person," Katie continued. "She taught Jeremy and Suzanne the real meaning of the first Thanksgiving." Katie turned to Mandy. "The Pilgrims and the Wampanoags realized they could all survive by working together and getting along. Jeremy and Suzanne got out of the corn maze by doing the same thing."

"How do you know what happened in that maze?" Suzanne asked Katie. "You weren't there."

Whoops. "Um . . . I . . . well . . . I could guess what happened," Katie said. "You and Jeremy are both here. And you're sitting next to each other without fighting."

"That's true," Ms. Sweet, Jeremy and Suzanne's teacher, said. "And they've been arguing all week."

"But now they even called off the corn-shucking contest," Mandy announced. "Suzanne just told me."

"We'll probably get it done faster if we just work together," Suzanne said.

Katie grinned.

Ms. Sweet smiled, too. "You are an excellent teacher, Patience," she said.

Patience smiled. "Thank you," she replied quietly.

"Right now she should go to her cottage and teach doll making," Miles said.

Patience looked at him. "Then I'm not . . ."

"Thou art not banished," Miles said.

Katie smiled. She didn't have to speak Pilgrim to know what that meant. Patience had her job back.

Hooray! Oops. She meant *Huzzah*!

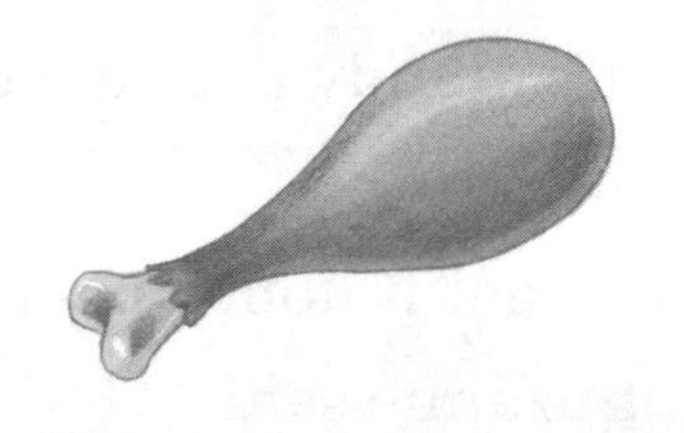

Chapter 13

Less than a week after her trip to the Good Morrow Village, Katie and her family were driving through New York City traffic in a modern day car. There were brightly lit signs flashing everywhere she looked. If the moon weren't in the sky, it would be easy to think it was daytime instead of night. That's how bright it was.

Usually, the city lights seemed magical to Katie. But tonight, Katie couldn't help being sad. Right now, her friends were eating delicious corn on the cob at the bonfire by the high school. Katie had spent hours helping to shuck corn last night. But now, here she was eating

Pre

soggy french fries in the backseat of the car. It just didn't seem fair.

While they drove through Central Park, Katie's mom said, "We're almost there. I can't wait to see them blow up the balloons. Alison said we can watch everything from their apartment window."

"We're lucky," Katie's dad said. "People wait in line for hours to see the balloons being blown up. All we have to do is look out the window."

Katie frowned. Watching people spend hours watching other people blowing up balloons didn't sound like a lot of fun. Not as much fun as a bonfire and corn on the cob, anyway.

Well, at least she would get to hang out with Emily. Emily was Katie's favorite cousin. She treated Katie like a friend instead of like a younger cousin. Emily was really cool. She had the greatest clothes and she got to wear makeup. Maybe if Katie was lucky, Emily would let her try her lip gloss and eye shadow.

Katie forced a smile to her lips and tried to make it stick.

"Okay, we're here!" Katie's dad announced as he parked the car on the street near Emily's house. Katie could see the big museum building on one side of the street and Central Park on the other.

Woof! Woof! Pepper leaped excitedly for the car door.

"Not so fast," Katie's mom said to the dog as they walked down the street to their relatives' apartment building. "Outside, you need to be on a leash in New York City." She reached up and attached a leash to Pepper's collar.

Suddenly Pepper didn't seem so happy anymore. Katie didn't blame him. But then, as soon as they got off the elevator and rang an apartment doorbell, Pepper perked up. So did Katie. It was hard not to feel happy once the door opened and you were being hugged and kissed by some of your favorite people in the world.

"Katie, I think you've grown a foot since I saw you," Aunt Alison said.

"Just an inch or two," Katie told her.

"Well, you look much more grown-up," Aunt Alison said.

Katie smiled at her aunt. It was amazing just how much she looked like Katie's dad. They both had the same wavy hair, dark eyes, and big smile. It was like they were the boy and girl versions of the same person.

"I have some really cool clothes for you," Emily added. "I put them away after I outgrew them. I think they'll fit you now."

Katie smiled—for real this time. New clothes that came from New York City. Wait until Suzanne heard about this!

Tweet! Suddenly a loud, shrill whistle came from the back of the apartment. Pepper's ears shot up. He ran toward the whistle and then stopped and looked around.

Emily started to giggle. "Oh no, Pepper," she said. "No one's calling you. That was just Parry."

"Parry?" Katie repeated. "Who's that?"

Emily smiled. "He's my new parakeet. He's really cute. He whistles a lot."

As if to prove it, Parry whistled again. Pepper's ears perked up, and he started running all around again, looking for who was calling him.

"That bird is going to make Pepper crazy," Katie's uncle Charlie said with a laugh. His chubby belly bounced up and down when he laughed.

Katie didn't think it was funny. Poor Pepper. He really thought someone was calling for him to come. Parry was teasing him.

"Katie, come over here," Emily said, pointing to a window. "You gotta see this."

"Okay," Katie said. She turned to her dog. "Pepper, come," she called sweetly.

Pepper stood there for a minute, making sure this wasn't another trick. Then he wagged his tail, and raced over to Katie.

"Look," Emily said.

Katie peered down at the street from the window. There were more people on the street than Katie had ever seen in her whole life. They were walking up and down the streets, looking at the balloons, and snapping pictures. Some kids sat on their dad's shoulders just so they could see. But Katie had no problem seeing all the action.

"Wow!" she exclaimed. "Those balloons are huge in person."

"It takes something like ten people holding on to the ropes to walk a balloon through the parade," Emily told her.

"Oh, look, there's a snowman balloon," Katie said excitedly. "And that balloon on the end is a big red star."

"I like to look at the ones that are only partly blown up, and try to guess what they're going to be," Emily said. "Like that white and brown one over there. What do you think that will be?"

Katie looked down. All she saw was a huge pile of brown and white cloth lying flat in the middle of the street. It didn't look like much of anything. At least not yet.

"Well, it's the same colors as Pepper, so maybe it will be a dog," Katie suggested.

Ding-dong. Just then, the doorbell rang. Katie looked up. Who else was coming to her cousin's house to watch the balloons being blown up? Her mom hadn't mentioned any other surprises.

"Emily, Sarah's here," Uncle Charlie called from the door.

Emily's friend Sarah burst into the room, and started talking right away. "It's crazy out there," Sarah said. "There are like a million people in the streets. And you can't get near any of the restaurants. I don't think anybody out there is actually from around here. They're all tourists and none of them know where they're going. Why do they all have to come here? We have enough people in this city already, and . . ."

Sarah stopped talking as soon as she spotted Katie sitting by the window with Emily. "Oh, sorry," she apologized. "You must be Emily's cousin from out of town. I didn't mean anything bad about tourists. I just . . ."

Katie stared at Sarah. She'd never heard anybody talk that fast before.

"Katie, this is my best friend Sarah," Emily said.

"Hi," Katie said.

"Hello," Sarah said. Then she turned her attention back to Emily. "Since there are lines a block long to get into any of our favorite restaurants, I brought takeout." She plopped a bag on a nearby coffee table. "I got some sandwiches. I wasn't sure which ones to get. So I just took a chance. And, of course, malteds from Mickey's."

"Oh, yum!" Emily said. "Katie, wait'll you have one. Mickey's malts are amazing!"

"I only brought two," Sarah said. "I forgot your little cousin was coming."

Katie frowned. She didn't like being called little cousin. *Younger* cousin maybe. Or even *shorter* cousin. But she was definitely not a little kid.

"That's okay," Emily told Katie. "We'll share. I'll just go get a glass."

As Emily walked off, Sarah asked Katie, "Is this your first Thanksgiving parade?"

Katie nodded.

"I've been to a bunch of them," Sarah said. "But this year I'm actually going to be *in* the parade. I can hardly wait. I can just picture myself walking in the middle of Broadway, with the crowds cheering and the music playing . . ."

"Wow!" Katie chimed in when Sarah stopped talking to take a breath. "Are you going to be one of those pretty girls singing on a float?"

Sarah shook her head. "No, I'm something much better," she said. "I'm going to be a clown. I get to walk next to the balloons and throw confetti at people to get the little kids all excited. The clowns are really the stars of the parade, I mean—"

"I thought the balloons were the most

important part," Katie broke in. "Aren't people already excited to be at a parade? Do they need clowns to get psyched up?"

Emily came back with two glasses and said, "This parade is all Sarah's been talking about for weeks now."

"Well, it's a huge deal," Sarah said. "About a thousand people tried out. And there are only fifty of us that got picked. We're going to be seen on TV by people all over the country. And being a clown is really cool. Some of us are on stilts and some of us do gymnastics routines. Wait until you see my backflip! Just look for the clown with the purple shoes and the yellow, orange, and purple pants. That will be me."

Katie took a huge gulp of her malted milkshake. Oooh! The cold drink made her brain freeze. What a headache!

Tweet! Tweet! Just then Parry flew by, perched on Emily's shoulder, and kept on whistling loudly.

Aroo! Pepper howled and started running all around the apartment. *Aroo! Aroo!*

And Sarah just kept talking and talking. *Blah. Blah. Blah.*

Katie sighed. If this was how New Yorkers celebrated Thanksgiving Eve, then all Katie could think was *thanks . . . but no thanks.*

Chapter 14

On Thanksgiving morning, there were about a million people standing outside on either side of Central Park West, waiting for the parade. Or at least it seemed that way to Katie. She'd never seen so many people in one place before.

It was also really, really cold outside. Katie's ears were freezing. If only she'd remembered to grab her hat and scarf. Some people had blankets wrapped around them like shawls. Some were drinking steaming mugs of chocolate. They were smart!

Since they were so near the entrance to Aunt Alison's apartment building, Katie asked, "Mom, can I run back upstairs to get my hat?"

Katie's mom thought for a minute. "I guess so. Uncle Charlie's still up there working on his special mashed potatoes. He'll let you in."

"You won't move or anything, right?" Katie asked nervously.

Her mom shook her head. "We'll be here when you get back. Standing right in front of the building."

"Okay," Katie said. "I'll only be a second."

And with that, Katie left and went into the apartment building. She smiled at Stan, the nice doorman who stood in the lobby and greeted everybody as they came in or went out.

"Good morning," Stan said. "Coming back for a hat?"

Katie nodded. "And a scarf, too."

"Good thinking," Stan told her. "It's a cold one today."

Katie began to wonder if it was as cold in Cherrydale as it was here. But then she decided that it was better not to think about Cherrydale anymore. Instead, she tried to think about those giant balloons. They were really cool. Especially the brown and white one that turned out to be a giant turkey, not a dog after all.

Katie stepped into the elevator and pushed the button for the fourth floor. As the doors shut, Katie felt a cool breeze blowing on the back of her neck.

Boy, she thought to herself. *It's even cold in the elevator.*

But there was something weird about the wind. For one thing, there were no windows in the elevator. And no fans, either. So where was the wind coming from? Even weirder, this wind was getting stronger and stronger. *And it was blowing only around Katie.*

That could mean only one thing. The magic wind had followed Katie all the way to New York City! And it was ready for a switcheroo!

"Oh no!" Katie cried out.

The magic wind began to pick up speed. It

blew harder and harder, circling around Katie like an icy tornado. She shut her eyes tight and tried hard not to cry.

And then it stopped. Just like that. The magic wind was gone. And so was Katie Carew. She'd turned into someone else. One . . . two . . . switcheroo!

But who?

Chapter 15

"Welcome to the Thanksgiving Day Parade!"

Katie heard a man's voice blaring from a loudspeaker. Right away everyone started clapping and whistling. Not far away she could hear a marching band starting to play. *Oompah-oompah* went a tuba.

Slowly, she blinked her eyes open and looked around. Katie was standing in the middle of the street. Uh-oh! Her parents wouldn't like that! And ahead of her was a huge, red, star-shaped balloon. One thing was for sure: Katie was back outside at the Thanksgiving Day Parade.

Okay, so now she knew *where* she was. But she still didn't know *who* she was.

Katie looked down. Her way-cool black and red cowboy boots were gone. Now she was wearing huge purple shoes. *Clown shoes.* And just above the shoes, Katie could see the bottom of her purple, yellow, and orange striped clown pants.

Katie started to get a funny feeling, and not a funny ha-ha feeling. It was a funny, *oh no!* feeling. Had she turned into Sarah? She felt the top of her head—yup, she was wearing a curly wig.

"Sarah, come on! What are you waiting for?" a clown with a red nose and orange hair called over to her. "We're supposed to be starting our routine."

That settled it. Katie was definitely Sarah. And right now, she was obviously supposed to be doing some sort of routine. The problem was, Katie didn't have a clue what the routine was.

Katie thought for a minute. Sarah had said something about confetti. Quickly, she reached into the pocket of the wacky clown pants. Sure enough, there was a pile of it in there. Katie pulled out a handful of confetti and threw it at the crowd.

"Yay!" the people in the crowd cheered as the confetti rained down on their heads.

Well, this wasn't so hard. Katie dipped into her other pocket and ran to the other side of the street where she tossed more confetti on a bunch of little kids. "More! More!" they shouted.

"What are you doing?" a clown with green hair shouted at Katie. "The confetti doesn't come out until 45th street."

"What street are we on now?" Katie asked him.

The green-haired clown looked at her strangely. "77th Street and Central Park West. What is wrong with you?"

Nothing was wrong with Katie—other than

the fact that she was in a strange body, in a strange city, performing in the middle of the street in a world-famous parade.

"You're supposed to do your backflip now," the orange-haired clown told Katie. "And then we go into the cartwheels."

Uh-oh. There was one small problem. Katie had never done a backflip in her life. And every time she tried to do cartwheels, she only got about a foot off the ground and then landed right on her rear end. This was *soooo* not good!

Katie looked around. Everywhere she turned, there were clowns in the street flipping, dancing, and spinning around and around in cartwheels. But Katie was just standing there. She had to do something. *Anything*.

So Katie decided to dance. She tapped her feet on the street, trying to remember some of the tap dancing moves her mom had taught her. But tap dancing was tough in size seventy-nine purple clown shoes.

“What are you doing?” the clown with green hair asked her. “Why are you making a fool of yourself on national television?”

What? Katie gulped. She’d forgotten all about the Thanksgiving Day Parade being on TV. But when she turned her head, there was a cameraman with a big TV camera perched on his shoulder.

"What are you doing?" Katie screamed at the cameramen. "The balloons are much more interesting than the clowns. Point your cameras up there."

All of the clowns stared at her.

"Sarah, what's wrong with you?" the orange-haired clown shouted. "We *want* to be on TV, remember?"

Katie gulped. She'd forgotten she was Sarah. But she remembered now. And no matter how annoying Sarah was, she didn't deserve to look like a fool on national TV. So Katie did the only gymnastics trick she knew. She bent over, curled her head into her chest, and did a somersault in the middle of the street.

As Katie stood up, she smiled proudly. In fact, she almost took a bow. Okay, so somersaults were pretty easy. But this one had been a pretty good somersault. She hadn't tipped to the side or anything.

The other clowns weren't impressed.

Instead they ignored her and started doing perfect cartwheels, backflips, and handstands in the street.

Katie sighed. A somersault seemed pretty babyish, considering what the other clowns were doing. So she tried a cartwheel of her own.

"One . . . two . . ." Katie counted as she tipped to her side. "Three . . ." She stretched out her arms and swooped down, just the way Becky Stern had told her was the correct way to do a cartwheel. Becky was awesome at gymnastics.

"Oomph!" Katie landed right on a yellow-haired clown, knocking her to the ground.

"Ouch!" the yellow-haired clown shouted.

"Out of the way!" the green-haired clown warned. He was doing front flips. Too late! He couldn't stop himself and tripped over the yellow-haired clown.

"Whoa!" the orange-haired clown screamed

as he backflipped right onto the green-haired clown.

"Hey, you're sitting on my head," the green-haired clown shouted.

Katie just sat on the ground in the middle of the clown pileup. They were all really angry behind their painted-on smiles.

Some people in the crowd started to laugh. But a few people began to boo. And then a few more. *Boooo!*

"That's not nice," Katie shouted back at them. "We're trying."

"The crowd is clearly not happy with the clown show," Katie heard one news reporter going on. "That one clown is causing a whole lot of trouble."

Uh-oh. Katie knew exactly who that trouble-causing clown was. It was her. Even though she was switcherooed into teenaged Sarah, Katie felt like a fourth-grade girl—one who was in big trouble. And so she did a very fourth-grade thing . . .

She started to run. *Fast.*

Katie had no idea where she was going. All she knew was she had to get out of there. Away from the crowds. Away from the cameras. And especially away from all those angry clowns.

Chapter 16

Katie didn't stop running through the crowd until she spotted a path. It led right into Central Park. There were no reporters or news cameras in the park. It was the perfect place to hide.

Or was it? Katie ran just a few steps down the path and then stopped. She didn't think being alone in Central Park was such a good idea.

From where she stood, Katie could see people lined up on the streets cheering. Balloons were flying high above the crowd. But Katie didn't see any building that looked like Emily's apartment. She didn't see the big museum that was right near Emily's building, either. In other words, she was lost!

A shiver went through her. It was really cold out. And her thin clown costume wasn't protecting her against the wind that had just started blowing against the back of her neck.

Katie looked up. Funny. The bare tree limbs weren't blowing at all. Neither were the brown fallen leaves on the ground. In fact, that wind didn't seem to be blowing anywhere except on Katie. Which could mean only one thing. The magic wind had returned!

The magic wind started picking up speed. It whirled and swirled all around Katie, moving faster and faster, and growing more and more powerful, until it was like a wild tornado. Her clown wig was about to fly off. Katie grabbed on to the sides of a rock to keep from being blown away.

And then it stopped. Just like that. The magic wind was gone. Katie Carew was back. And so was Sarah. She was standing there,

right next to Katie. And, boy, was she confused.

"What am I doing here?" Sarah asked Katie. She stopped for a second. "What are *you* doing here? You shouldn't be alone in Central Park."

Katie didn't know what to say. She couldn't just tell Sarah about the magic wind. She wouldn't believe her if she did, anyway.

"I'm not alone," Katie said finally. "I'm with you."

Sarah looked at her strangely. "I shouldn't be here, either. I'm supposed to be in the parade with the other clowns . . ." Sarah stopped for a minute. "Oh no," she said quietly. "Did I really do something as babyish as a somersault in the middle of Central Park West?"

Katie wasn't sure where she'd done the somersault, but she knew she had done one.

"It was a good somersault," Katie said. "Almost perfect. You didn't tilt or anything."

Sarah shook her head. "Are you kidding?" she asked. "I just made a complete fool of myself in front of the entire country. Everyone is going to be making fun of me."

That made Katie feel horrible. If there was one thing she couldn't stand, it was being made fun of. And now that was going to be happening to Sarah. And it was all Katie's fault.

"No one will make fun of you," Katie said. "Clowns are supposed to be funny. And you were funny."

But Sarah didn't believe her. "I was weird. *Really* weird. I mean, who does a somersault in a parade?"

Katie didn't know how to answer that. Sarah had just called her weird. Right to her face! But of course Sarah didn't know she was calling Katie weird. She thought she was talking about herself. So Katie couldn't really get mad.

"Look, I've got to get back to the parade," Sarah said. "I need to catch up to the other clowns."

Sarah leaped up and started to run out of the park. Katie sat there for a moment, watching her. And then she started to cry.

Sarah stopped running. She turned around and stared at Katie. "What are you crying about?" she asked.

"I don't know how to get back to Emily's," Katie said between her cries. "I don't even know where I am."

Sarah sighed heavily. "All right, come on," she said. "I'll drop you by Emily's building and then I'll try to catch up with the parade."

Katie stood up. "Th-thank you," she said.

Sarah rolled her eyes. "Tourists," she groaned. "You guys should never go out by yourselves."

Katie knew Sarah was right. Now if she could only convince the magic wind of that!

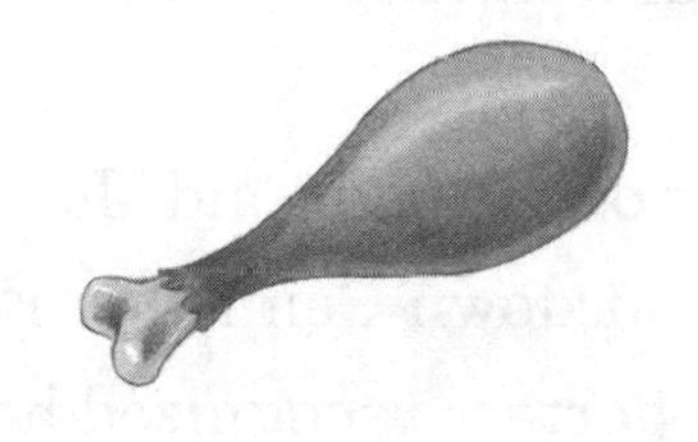

Chapter 17

Sarah didn't say anything to Katie as they walked back toward the parade together. Instead, she just kept repeating the word *somersault* over and over again, and shaking her head. Katie really hoped the other clowns would be nice to Sarah.

A few minutes later, Katie spotted the big museum that was near Emily's apartment building. Woo-hoo! She would be back with her parents, her aunt, and her cousin any second now. And luckily, there was still plenty of parade to see.

Katie saw her cousin. She started jumping

up and down and waving. "Look, Sarah! There's Emily."

"Well, bye now," Sarah said. Just as she was about to take off down Central Park West, one of the news reporters recognized her.

"There she is!" one newscaster shouted out. "That's the clown that messed up everything!"

Sarah gasped. "Oh no!"

The reporter started running toward her, with his microphone in hand.

Sarah tried to take off. But Katie grabbed the back of her clown costume. She'd just gotten one of her great ideas.

"Sarah, wait!" Katie shouted. A second later, the reporter and his news crew was shoving a microphone in Sarah's face.

"So, what happened out there?" the news reporter demanded. "You were acting crazy in the parade, and then you just disappeared."

"Well . . . I . . ." Sarah didn't know what to say to him.

Katie's eyes grew wide. It was probably the first time that had ever happened to Sarah. But Katie also knew it wasn't funny. No one wanted to be embarrassed, especially in front of a news crew.

"She was helping me!" Katie said, jumping in front of the camera. "I got lost. I'm not from around here. I was heading into Central Park."

"Why were you going into the park?" the reporter asked Katie.

Katie couldn't exactly tell the reporter that a magic wind had blown her in there. So instead she said, "I made a wrong turn. And Sarah was so worried about me that she left the parade to help me out."

Sarah stared curiously at Katie. She had no idea what she was talking about. But Katie didn't stop to explain. She just kept talking to the reporter.

"I was really glad when Sarah showed up," Katie continued. "She saved me. I mean it's so crowded here. I would have never found my mom and dad on my own."

"Wow! You're a real hero," the news reporter said to Sarah.

Suddenly, Sarah found her voice again. "Well, I'm a New Yorker, and she's not," she said proudly. "So I knew I had to help her. We New Yorkers are very helpful people."

The news reporter smiled into the camera. "And there you have it, folks. A message to all of you who are thinking about visiting New York. Come! New Yorkers are here to help."

Katie started to giggle. It didn't seem like Sarah would be happy with more tourists in New York. But at least she didn't look embarrassed anymore. In fact, she was smiling for the cameras. Sarah was right. She had just become one of the stars of the parade.

Thanks to Katie, of course.

Chapter 18

"Could you please pass the mashed potatoes, Aunt Alison?" Katie asked.

Katie's aunt passed the huge bowl of Uncle Charlie's special mashed potatoes down to the other end of the table where Katie was sitting. Katie plopped a big spoonful onto her plate and dug in. "Your tofurkey was delicious," Katie told her aunt. "It was so nice of you to have it for me."

"Wow. Am I full," Katie's mom said.

"I think I'm going to pop a button on these pants if I eat another bite," Uncle Charlie added.

"I bet that's why the Pilgrims called

their big meals groaning tables," Katie said. "Because after a while, everyone gets so full, they start groaning."

"I wouldn't doubt it," Katie's dad agreed.

"I know one person who's finally stopped groaning," Emily said. "Sarah. She called me after the parade, and I've never heard her so happy. She said she's going to be on three news shows tonight."

"I still don't understand how you got lost, Katie," Aunt Alison said. "We were standing right in front of the building. It was like you blew right past us."

Katie tried hard not to laugh. That was *exactly* what it was like. But she could never tell her aunt that. Instead she said, "Well I'm glad I got back in time to see the rest of the parade. Especially the big sleigh carrying Santa."

"That means Christmas can't be far off," Uncle Charlie said. "Are you guys planning a vacation for Christmas?"

"Oh no," Katie's dad said. "We're spending that holiday in Cherrydale."

Katie smiled. She was glad her dad had said that. Christmas was definitely the kind of holiday you wanted to spend at home.

Still, this Thanksgiving had turned out a lot better than she'd ever expected. The parade had been really exciting to watch. Her cousin Emily had given her some really cool clothes. And Thanksgiving dinner was delicious.

Best of all, Katie was surrounded by her family. They were all laughing, joking, and having a really good time.

Just then, Katie felt a cold wind blowing on the back of her neck. Oh no! Could the magic wind be back? Right now? *In the middle of Thanksgiving dinner?*

"Charlie, can you shut that window?" Aunt Alison called from across the table. "It's getting chilly in here."

Phew. It was just an ordinary, late

November wind. The kind of wind that doesn't switcheroo you.

That meant Katie could stay Katie. At least for now. And that was definitely something to be thankful for.

Eat Like They Did at the First Thanksgiving!

Katie and her friends had a lot of fun during their visit to the Good Morrow Village. One of the best things about the field trip was that the kids could eat just like the Wampanoags and the Pilgrims did.

One of Katie's favorite dishes at the groaning board was called stewed pompion. It's a dish made with pumpkins or squash that's easy to make and delicious to eat. Here's a modern stewed pompion recipe you can try at home.

This recipe makes four servings.

You will need:

2 medium acorn squash (about 2 ½ pounds), peeled and cut into squares

1 cup 1% low fat milk

3 tablespoons butter

3 teaspoons cider vinegar

2 teaspoons ground ginger

½ teaspoon salt

Here's what you do:

1. Ask an adult to help you peel, cut, and boil the acorn squash in a large pot of water, until the squash is soft.
2. Have an adult drain the boiled squash.
3. Mash the squash.
4. Add the butter, vinegar, ginger, and salt.
5. Stir until everything is completely mixed.
6. Serve warm.

Kevin's favorite dish was one the Wampanoags liked to make. It's called succotash. The succotash in the village didn't have any tomatoes, but it sure was tasty. Here's a modern succotash recipe that you are sure to love making—and eating!

This recipe makes four servings.

You will need:

3 tablespoons butter

½ cup chopped red pepper

2 cups frozen or canned corn, drained

2 cups frozen lima beans

¼ cup water

¼ teaspoon salt

¼ teaspoon pepper

Here's what you do:

1. Ask an adult to help you heat one tablespoon of butter in a saucepan.
2. Work with an adult to chop the red pepper and cook it in the melted butter until tender. This should take about one minute.
3. Stir in the corn, lima beans, and water.
4. Simmer the mixture for three minutes.
5. Stir in the remaining two tablespoons of butter and season with salt and pepper.
6. Serve warm.

About the Author

Nancy Krulik is the author of more than 150 books for children and young adults, including three *New York Times* best sellers. She lives in New York City with her husband, composer Daniel Burwasser, their children, Amanda and Ian, and Pepper, a chocolate and white spaniel mix. When she's not busy writing the *Katie Kazoo, Switcheroo* series, Nancy loves swimming, reading, and going to the movies.

About the Illustrators

John & Wendy have illustrated all of the *Katie Kazoo* books, but when they're not busy drawing Katie and her friends, they like to paint, take photographs, travel, and play music in their rock 'n' roll band. They live and work in Brooklyn, New York.

Katie Kazoo, Switcheroo

Visit **www.katiekazoo.com** for fun activities, a chance to join the Katie Kazoo Classroom Crew, and to find out about Katie's reading challenge!